Tiddalick the Thirsty Frog

A play based on an
Australian Aboriginal story

Retold by Mark Carthew
Illustrated by Greg Rogers

Collins

Characters

Tiddalick (non-speaking)

Readers 1, 2, 3, 4, 5

Kangaroo

Emu

Dingo

Snake

Wombat

Frill-necked Lizard

Kookaburra

Cockatoos

Turn to page **21** for Sound and Stage Tips

Sound Makers

These parts can be played by any number of students. The sound makers improvise sounds on musical instruments or everyday objects to match the actions in the story.

 Loud bullfrog croaking

 Mountains rumbling and trees shaking

 Tiddalick hopping

 Tiddalick drinking and burping

 Sun beating down

 Kangaroo bounding

 Cockatoos squawking

 Wombat waddling and animals marching

 Lizard strutting and dancing

 Tiddalick snoring

 Wombat balancing

 Snake hissing and slithering

 Leapfrogging hops and boings

 Wings flapping

 Kookaburra laughing

 Earthquake rumbling

 Water gushing and flooding

 Small frog croaking

Tiddalick the Thirsty Frog

Scene 1   Outback Australia

(Tiddalick sits in the middle of the stage. The other animals graze quietly in the background.)

Reader 1:   In times long ago, when the deserts were covered in green grass and the rivers were full and flowing …

Reader 2:   There lived a large frog called Tiddalick.

Reader 3:   He was the largest of all the frogs.

Reader 4: The biggest and fattest frog ever.

Reader 5: So very big, that next to him the tallest trees looked like twigs and the highest mountains looked like small hills.

Reader 1: When Tiddalick croaked …

the mountains shook and the animals trembled in fear.

Reader 2: Now, being such a big frog, Tiddalick was very thirsty.

Reader 3: One morning, Tiddalick went to the river to have a drink.

(Tiddalick hops forward.)

Reader 4: He drank so much that the river ran dry.

Reader 5: But the greedy frog was still thirsty.

Reader 1:   So he hopped over the mountains and trees …

Reader 2:   And he drank up all the water from the billabongs and lakes as well! *(Tiddalick drinks the water, then burps.)*

Reader 3: Soon there was no water left anywhere in the land.

Reader 4: Tiddalick was now so big and fat that he could hardly move.

Reader 5: The hot sun beat down and dried out the earth.

Reader 1: And with all the water gone, the land soon began to die.

Reader 2: Kangaroo decided enough was enough.

Kangaroo: *(Bounding forward.)* We need a meeting of all the animals!

(All the animals mumble and nod in agreement.)

Reader 3: So the cockatoos flew out over the land to spread the news.

(Cockatoos fly around.)

Cockatoos: Squawk! Squawk! Squawk!

Scene 2   A Dry Riverbed

(Animals gather around Kangaroo and Emu.)

Emu: *(Scratching at the riverbed.)* We must make Tiddalick give back the water or we will die of thirst!

All: Mumble, grumble, mumble.

Reader 4:   Everyone agreed, but no one knew how to make Tiddalick give back the water.

Dingo: Grrrr. We will make him give it back!

Reader 5: But all the animals agreed that Tiddalick was much too strong.

(Animals shake their heads and look sad.)

They all stood silently and thought.

Reader 1: At last, old Wombat spoke.

Wombat: If only we could make Tiddalick laugh, then all the water will run back out.

All: Good idea, Wombat. Let's go!

Reader 2: So the animals followed Wombat and marched bravely off towards Tiddalick's resting place.

Scene 3   Tiddalick's Resting Place

Reader 3:   Finally, they found Tiddalick sitting beside an empty river.

Reader 4:   Tiddalick slowly opened one giant eye and looked at them all without speaking.

Reader 5:   One by one, the animals tried to make Tiddalick laugh.

Reader 1:   Frill-necked Lizard puffed out and strutted to and fro, dancing right under Tiddalick's eye!

Reader 2: But Tiddalick just looked bored and started to fall asleep.

Reader 3: Wombat stood on his head, but Tiddalick did not even blink an eye!

Snake: *Hiss …* Let me try! *Hiss …*

Reader 4: Snake made lots of strange and silly shapes. He even tied himself into a knot! But Tiddalick only yawned.

Reader 5: Kangaroo and Emu played leapfrog together.

Reader 1: And when this didn't work, Kangaroo did leapfrogs over all the animals!

Reader 2: But Tiddalick just sat there and looked bored.

Reader 3: Soon all the animals had tried every trick they knew.

Reader 4: They all sat down, feeling very sad.

Reader 5: It seemed like they would never get their water back.

Reader 1: Suddenly, a feathery shape landed beside them.

Reader 2:   It was Kookaburra!

Reader 3:   He waddled up to Tiddalick
and looked long and hard at him,
with one eye and then the other.

Reader 4:   Then he began to laugh.

Kookaburra: Koo-hoo-hoo-hoo-hoo-ha-ha-ha-ha-ha!

Reader 5:   He laughed so long and so
loud that all the other animals
started laughing as well.

All: Koo-hoo-hoo-hoo-hoo-ha-ha-ha-ha-ha!

Reader 1: Kookaburra was still laughing when a deep rumble started inside Tiddalick.

Reader 2: The sound grew louder and louder …

Reader 3: Suddenly, Tiddalick's mouth opened and he burst out laughing!

Reader 4: A mighty rush of water came gushing out of Tiddalick's mouth.

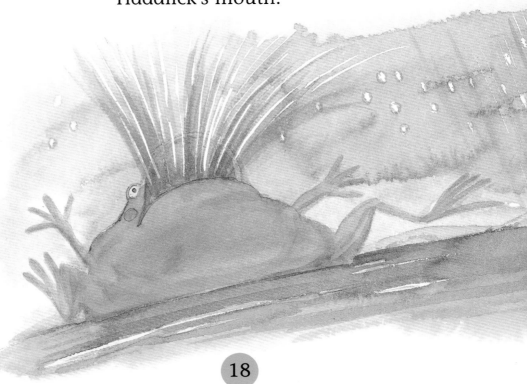

Reader 5: The animals ran to escape as water flooded in all directions.

All: *(Animal sounds.)* Arrggh! Squawk! Hiss!

Reader 1: The thirsty earth soaked up all the water and soon the land was green again.

Reader 2: Tiddalick shrank like a burst balloon and slunk away to hide.

Reader 3:   All the animals drank from the billabongs and rivers once again.

Reader 4:   And Kookaburra …

All: He's still laughing!

Kookaburra: Koo-hoo-hoo-hoo-hoo-ha-ha-ha-ha-ha!

(In some versions of this Australian Aboriginal story, it is an eel that finally makes the greedy Tiddalick laugh.)

Sound and Stage Tips

About This Play

Tiddalick the Thirsty Frog is a 'sound story' or radio play that you can read with your friends in a group or perform in front of an audience. Sound stories use sound effects to help tell the story.

Before you start reading, choose a part you would like to read and the sound effects you would like to create. There are fifteen main parts in this play: Tiddalick (non-speaking), Readers 1–5, Kangaroo, Emu, Dingo, Snake, Wombat, Frill-necked Lizard, Kookaburra and at least two Cockatoos. You will also need a number of sound makers, who could be other students in the class. Make sure you have readers and sound makers for all the parts.

If you have a smaller group, the readers could double as the sound makers. For a larger performance, you could have as many animal characters and sound makers as you like!

Reading the Play

It's a good idea to read the play through to yourself before you read it as part of a group. It is best to have your own book, as that will help you too. As you read the play through, think about the sorts of voices and sounds that might help present this story to an audience.

Rehearsing the Play

Rehearse the play a few times before you perform it for others. It's great fun to record your rehearsals, and especially your final performance.

When you rehearse *Tiddalick the Thirsty Frog*, it is important to practise matching the sound effects with the actions in the story. Acting in time with the sounds will really help the story to come alive!

Using Your Voice

Remember to speak out clearly and be careful not to read too quickly! Speak more slowly than you do when you're speaking to your friends. Keep in mind that the audience is hearing your words for the first time.

In *Tiddalick the Thirsty Frog*, the sound effects and the story told by the readers are great fun to hear. Remember to look at the audience and at the other performers, making sure everyone can hear what you are saying and creating.

Creating Sound Effects (FX)

Sound effects are an essential part of a sound story or radio play. The picture icons in the book  indicate the best place to make the sound effects. Think of different ways of creating the matching sound pictures.

Musical instruments or normal everyday objects can be used for making sound effects. For example, you could use a glockenspiel to make the tinkling sounds of the Lizard strutting and dancing. Have fun and experiment with your choices before you perform the play!

Sets and Props

Once you have read the play, make a list of the things you will need, especially for all the sound makers! Sound stories are normally performed without sets and props. However, if you wish to have the animals act the story as it is told, here are some ideas to help your performance.

- Backdrop of the desert
- Trees and rocks
- Dry riverbed
- Sound making instruments/objects

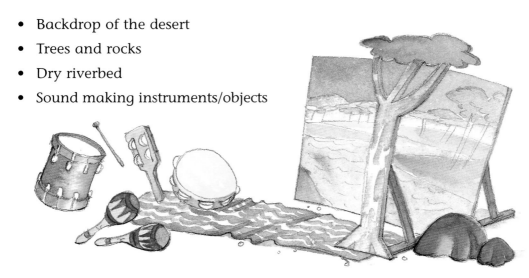

Costumes

Costumes are not required for *Tiddalick the Thirsty Frog* as the story is told in the sounds and in the readers' lines. However, if you decide to have performers acting or miming the animals' roles, you may like to make simple costumes for the following:

- Kangaroo, Emu, Frill-necked Lizard, Dingo, Wombat, Snake, Kookaburra and the Cockatoos
- Five Readers, who could also dress up as Australian animals

Have fun!

❧ Ideas for guided reading ❧

Learning objectives: explore narrative order; identify and map out main stages of the story; prepare, read and perform playscripts; take different roles in groups

Curriculum links: Science: Solids, liquids and how they can be separated

Interest words: Aboriginal, Kookaburra, Outback, Tiddalick, billabongs, radio play

Resources: percussion instruments, digital or tape recorder

Casting: (1–5) Readers 1-5
(6) All the animals (All) Cockatoos

Getting started

- Explain that this is a play based on an Australian Aboriginal story. Ask children for their ideas about the Australian Outback and the creatures that live there.
- Look at p2 together and read the names of the characters. Discuss each creature's main characteristics.
- Walk through scene one. Notice the conventions of the playscript, including the order in which the readers speak, and the use of symbols for sound FX.
- Read scene one together. Model how to narrate the play using the storytelling language for effect, e.g. *In times long ago... .*

Reading and responding

- At the end of scene one, ask the children to discuss what might happen in this traditional tale. Encourage them to take turns and to listen to each other's ideas.
- Read scene two (pp11–12). Establish that each creature is going to try to make Tiddalick laugh. Ask them to take turns to suggest how their creature may make the huge frog laugh.
- Discuss which creature is most likely to be successful. Praise them for listening to each other and using their knowledge of their creature to make suggestions.
- Continue reading the play together to the end. Help children to create interest by modelling how to read with expression.

Returning to the book

- Ask children, in pairs, to walk through the play and identify the main stages in this story.